WELCOME TO
PASSPORT TO READING
A beginning reader's ticket to a brand-new world!

Every book in this program is designed to build read-along and read-alone skills, level by level, through engaging and enriching stories. As the reader turns each page, he or she will become more confident with new vocabulary, sight words, and comprehension.

These PASSPORT TO READING levels will help you choose the perfect book for every reader.

READING TOGETHER
Read short words in simple sentence structures together to begin a reader's journey.

READING OUT LOUD
Encourage developing readers to sound out words in more complex stories with simple vocabulary.

READING INDEPENDENTLY
Newly independent readers gain confidence reading more complex sentences with higher word counts.

READY TO READ MORE
Readers prepare for chapter books with fewer illustrations and longer paragraphs.

This book features sight words from the educator-supported Dolch Sight Word List. Readers will become more familiar with these commonly used vocabulary words, increasing reading speed and fluency.

For more information, please visit www.passporttoreadingbooks.com, where each reader can add stamps to a personalized passport while traveling through story after story!

Enjoy the journey!

Little, Brown and Company

Hachette Book Group
237 Park Avenue, New York, NY 10017
Visit our website at www.lb-kids.com

Little, Brown and Company is a division of Hachette Book Group, Inc.
The Little, Brown name and logo are trademarks of Hachette Book Group, Inc.

The publisher is not responsible for websites (or their content)
that are not owned by the publisher.

First Edition: April 2012

ISBN 978-0-316-18871-5

10 9 8 7 6 5 4 3 2 1

CW

Printed in the United States of America

Licensed by: Hasbro

TRANS FORMERS PRIME

MEET TEAM PRIME

Adapted by Kirsten Mayer
Based on the pilot written by Duane Capizzi

LITTLE, BROWN AND COMPANY
New York Boston

Attention, Transformers fans!

Look for these items when you read this book.

Can you spot them all?

HOLOGRAM

SEDAN

COMPUTER SCREEN

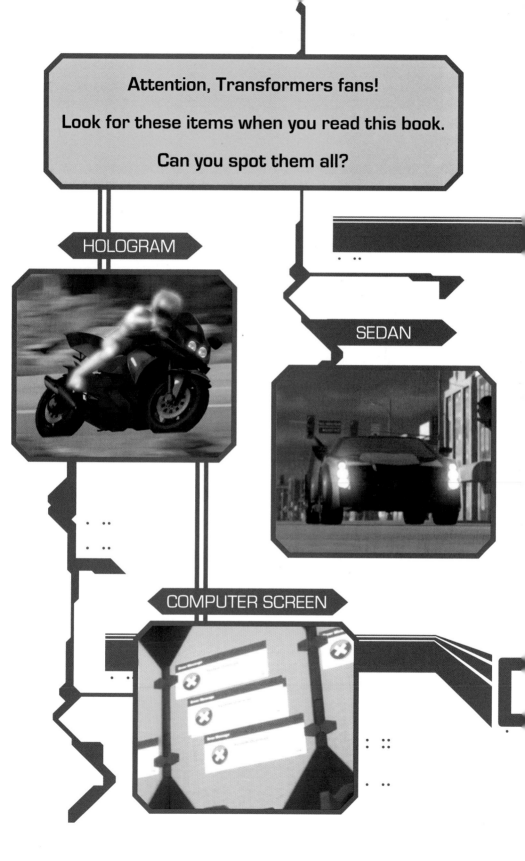

Optimus Prime and his Autobot team
live on Earth.
They patrol the planet
to defend it against the evil Decepticons.

Optimus Prime is the leader of the team.
"We must protect humankind,"
he tells his friends.
Optimus can change into a semitruck
to blend in on Earth.

Another member of the team is Arcee.
She cruises the streets as a motorcycle
and projects a hologram of a rider
so no one suspects anything.

Autobot rule number one is
to keep a low profile.
While on patrol, Arcee is followed.
She parks at a restaurant to hide in plain sight.

A boy named Jack sees Arcee
and thinks she is a normal bike.
Jack gets on to pretend for a moment
that he owns such a cool motorcycle.

Two dark sedans slowly pull up.
They are Decepticons.
The sedans rev their engines and
roar toward Arcee.

"Oh, no!" yells Arcee.

She takes off down the street
with Jack still on board.
The Decepticons race after them.

"Whoa!" Jack cries in surprise.

"Do not let go!" orders Arcee.

"Who said that?" asks Jack.

He has never heard of a talking bike.

13

A yellow-and-black car drives up and honks.
It is the Autobot named Bumblebee.
He lost his voice in a battle long ago
and now communicates without speaking.
"Is that a friend of yours?" asks Jack.
"Family," answers Arcee.

The sedans are gaining on them.

Arcee jumps a bridge and screeches to a stop...

right in front of a boy named Raf!

Raf is playing with a remote-control car.

Arcee and Bumblebee quickly shift forms.
They turn to fight the Decepticons,
who have changed from sedans into robots.

Jack and Raf run down the street to safety.

Raf asks, "What are they?"

Jack answers, "Talking cars that turn into robots—
or maybe the other way around."

Bumblebee and Arcee beat back the 'Cons.

Arcee reports over the radio.
"Arcee to Optimus!" she says.
"The 'Cons are back!
They would be scrap metal by now,
but some humans got in the way."

"Humans?" cries Optimus Prime.
"If our enemies saw them with you,
the humans will be in great danger.
You must bring them back."

Arcee and Bumblebee head out
to look for Raf and Jack.
They find the boys walking together.
Bumblebee drives up to Raf
and honks his horn.
The car door pops open.

"He wants me to get in," says Raf.

"Just you? How do you know?" asks Jack.

Raf understands Bumblebee.

"Your ride is over there," says Raf.

Arcee is nearby in motorcycle form.

Someone else sees Arcee, too.

A girl named Miko watches them.

She sees Arcee shift into a robot.

Arcee speaks to Jack.

"Come with me," she says.

"It is for your safety."

"Duh, go with her!" shouts Miko.

Arcee sees the girl.

Now that Miko has seen an Autobot,

she has to keep the secret, too.

"Oh, brother," says Arcee. "Come on."

She tells Miko to come with them.

"Woo-hoo!" yells Miko.

The girl cannot wait to ride such a cool bike.

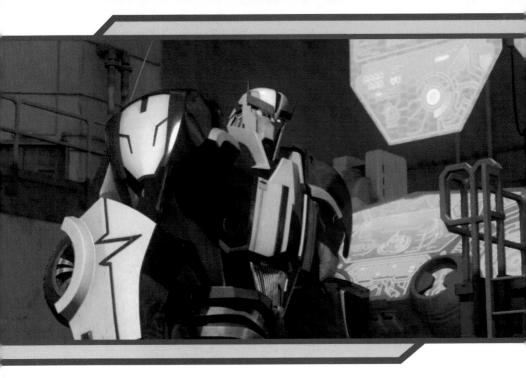

The Autobots have a secret base
in the middle of the Nevada desert.
Ratchet is the Autobot who operates
the GroundBridge transport system,
which allows the Autobots to go anywhere
on the planet in just moments.

When Arcee and Bumblebee
return to the base,
Ratchet, Bulkhead, and Optimus are surprised
to see three humans with them.

Miko marches right up to Bulkhead.
He is a huge Autobot who is very strong
and can turn into an off-road vehicle.
"I am Miko. What are you?
Are you a car? I bet you are a truck."

"We are autonomous robotic organisms from the planet Cybertron," says Optimus. "We are here to protect Earth from Decepticons."

"Why are they here?" asks Jack.

"Our home planet was destroyed,"
Optimus explains.

"The Decepticons wish to take over Earth.
It is best that you remain under our watch."

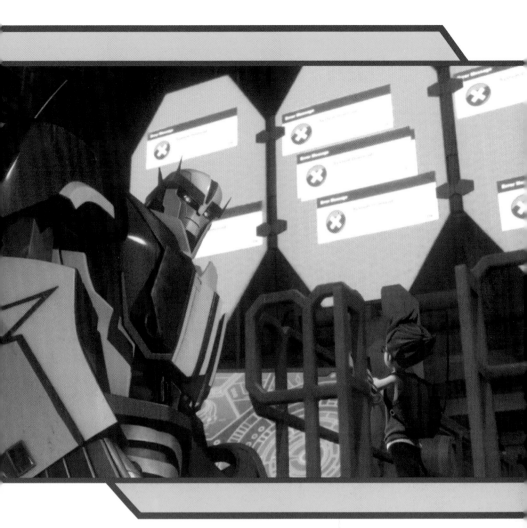

"They have no protective shells!"

Ratchet grumbles.

His computer screen shows an error message.

"I think I can fix that," says Raf.

Ratchet is amazed to see

Raf quickly fix the computer.

"These humans are now part of Team Prime," says Optimus Prime.

"And Team Prime is a family."

"Awesome!" yells Miko.

Jack, Raf, and Miko cannot wait to see what adventures lie ahead!

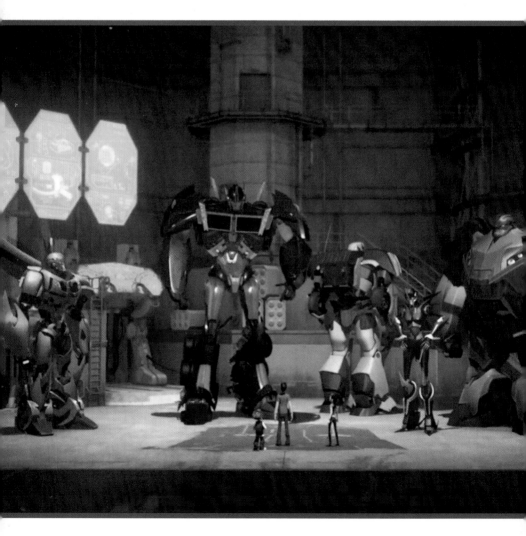